Dream Dogs

PEPPER

With special thanks to Lucy Courtenay and Nellie Ryan

First published in Great Britain by HarperCollins *Children's Books* 2010
HarperCollins Children's Books is a division of HarperCollins*Publishers* Ltd,
77-85 Fulham Palace Road, Hammersmith, London W6 8JB

The HarperCollins *Children's Books* website address is
www.harpercollins.co.uk

2

Dream Dogs : Pepper
Text copyright © HarperCollins 2010
Illustrations copyright © HarperCollins 2010

ISBN-13 978 0 00 732034 9

Printed and bound in England by
Clays Ltd, St Ives plc

PEPPER

Aimee Harper

HarperCollins *Children's Books*

Special thanks to
The Happy Dog Grooming Parlour, Farnham

Introducing...

Name: Pepper

Breed: Norfolk Terrier

Age: 3

Colour: Brown

Likes: Bones, cuddles, smelly blankets, walks

Dislikes: Vacuum cleaners, white vans, sitting still

Favourite game: Hide-and-seek

Most likely to be mistaken for: A large scrubbing brush

One

What a Mess!

"Come on, Louie!" Bella called. She jumped with excitement. "Mum wants *both* of us to switch on the sign!"

Bella's brother Louie put down his football and joined Bella by the light switch.

"Ready," he said, grinning up at her.

Bella looked out of the big glass window.
She could see her mum, Suzi, standing outside.
Her heart thumped. The Dream Dogs sign was
about to light up for the first time!

"Go!" Suzi called through the window.

Bella and Louie pressed the switch together.

Louie stared around the room. "Nothing
happened," he said in disappointment.

Bella giggled and pointed to where their
mum was jumping up and down on the
pavement with her thumbs up. "The Dream
Dogs sign is *outside*, remember?"

"Oh yeah," Louie said. "I forgot."

Suzi flung open the door and beckoned Bella
and Louie outside. "Come and see, kids!" she

said. "It looks fantastic!"

Pepper sat up in his basket and pricked up one brown ear. The other ear hung loose and floppy as usual. Bella bent down and ruffled his fuzzy head.

"Let's go, Pepper!" she said, kissing him on the nose. Picking him up, Bella tucked him under her arm. He fitted like a neat brown parcel, and tried to lick her ear. Pepper loved cuddles. He liked putting his paws round Bella's neck and hugging her.

Bella dashed outside and joined her mum

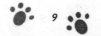

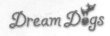

and Louie on the pavement. The curly pink

Dream Dogs sign over the window of their new

dog-grooming parlour was shining brightly in

the dark afternoon. It was the coolest thing

that Bella had ever seen!

"Well, kids," Suzi said happily, "we've done it. Our dream is finally coming true. This time next week, the best dog parlour in the world will be open for business!"

Bella felt her smile wobbling at the edges. The sign was lovely, but the view through Dream Dogs' window was *awful*. And anyone who walked past would see!

There were pots of paint and piles of boxes everywhere. A heap of rubbish bags lay in the middle of the floor. The walls were still a sludgy green colour from the florist's that had been here before they moved in, and the carpet was worn.

"Brilliant, Mum!" said Louie.

Pepper barked like he was agreeing.

Bella gulped. "Really good," she said, trying to sound happy.

"You don't sound very excited," Suzi said in surprise. "I thought you'd love it!"

Bella swallowed. "Sorry," she said. "It's just – well – nothing is ready, is it? And we're supposed to open on Saturday!"

"Everything will be fine," Suzi promised. "You're such a worrier, Bella!"

Bella knew it was true. She *did* worry about things. She couldn't help it.

She followed her mum and her little brother back inside. Suzi switched on the radio in the corner and Dream Dogs filled with funky music.

Pushing the rubbish bags to one side, Suzi and Louie started dancing.

"Come on!" Suzi laughed, reaching out her hand to Bella. "Dance with us! Let's celebrate!"

Bella grinned. She loved this song. Louie was spinning round like a top, getting dizzy. Putting Pepper down, Bella took her mum's hand. Suddenly it didn't matter that everyone could see them from out in the street. Pepper joined in, racing round in circles like Louie and barking.

"Woo-oo-oof!" Louie sang.

"Woof woof!" Pepper barked back. Bella couldn't help laughing.

When the song finished, Suzi flopped down on top of some boxes. Pepper and Louie were so dizzy that they both fell over. Bella put her arm round her mum's waist as Pepper struggled to his feet, jumped up on a box and licked her chin.

"I've taken some bookings for next week," said Suzi, pulling Bella in for a cuddle. "I couldn't believe it when the phone started ringing yesterday. That advertisement in the paper was a brilliant idea."

Bella gulped. Her mum was taking bookings

already? But there was still so much to *do!*

"What if Dream Dogs isn't ready?" she said, biting her lip.

Suzi took Bella's hands. "It will be," she insisted. "Trust me, love."

Bella gazed into her mum's eyes. They were kind and warm and brown, just like Pepper's. Pepper wriggled in between them and rested his head on Bella's lap.

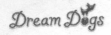
Suddenly the box they were sitting on broke. Towels and plastic containers fell out, adding to the mess on the floor. Pepper yelped and ran through the door which led up from the parlour to the flat upstairs. Louie roared with laughter, and so did Suzi.

But Bella didn't.

There's no way Dream Dogs will be ready to open next week, she thought with a sigh as she bent down to pick up the mess. *Mum must be crazy!*

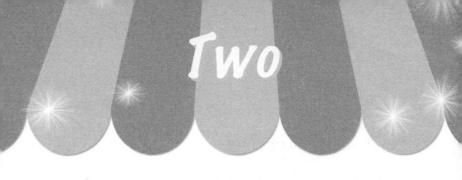

Two

A New Friend

Bella opened her eyes and stared at the ceiling.

For a minute, she couldn't remember where she

was. Then it all came back to her. *Sandmouth.*

Their new home town!

She sat up and sniffed the air. It smelled

salty. Dream Dogs and their flat were only two

streets away from the beach! She felt a rush of excitement that blew away all of yesterday's worries. You couldn't be upset near the sea.

"Are you up yet, you two?" her mum called from across the hallway. "School today, remember?"

This was Bella and Louie's second week at their new school, Cliffside Primary. Bella jumped up and pulled on her uniform. Her new school sweatshirt was still soft and fleecy, and she liked the purple colour. She felt a bit nervous though. Everyone had been nice to her last week, but she didn't have a best friend yet. She really hoped she'd find one soon.

"Purple's for girls," Louie grumbled, getting

out of his bed on the other side of the room and putting on his uniform like it was made of slime.

"Maybe we should start calling you Lulu!" Bella said cheekily.

She pulled her head through her sweatshirt and reached for her hairbrush. Soon, her chin-length brown hair was straight and neat. Louie didn't bother with his brush. His hair stuck up like hedgehog bristles, no matter what he did.

"Pepper's determined to catch his first wave today," Suzi told Bella and Louie as she put some bread into the toaster.

Cliffside Primary was down by the seafront.

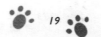

They had to walk along the beach to get there.
Pepper hadn't got used to the sea yet, and
chased the waves as if they were rabbits. But
he hadn't got his feet wet once. Bella patted
him on the head.

"You were a bit rubbish at catching waves
last week, weren't you, Peps?" she grinned.
"Were the waves too fast, or just too scary?"

Pepper sneezed and licked Bella's hand.

The toast popped up. Suzi hooked out the slices with two long pink-painted fingernails. All of Suzi's clothes were pink today, Bella realised. Even the silk scarf in her long brown hair.

"You're very pink today, Mum," Bella said.

"Pink is the Dream Dogs colour," Suzi said dreamily, admiring her nails. "I'm going to be a walking advertisement for our parlour. In fact, I'm thinking of getting some Dream Dogs T-shirts printed. Pink ones, of course, with the lettering just like our sign. What do you think?"

"*I'm* not wearing one," Louie said.

Suzi stroked Louie's bristly hair. "I was thinking more like a uniform for me to wear in the parlour," she explained. Then she gasped.

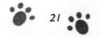

"Overalls! Yes. Pink overalls, with the Dream Dogs logo. Then I can get as wet as a fish and it won't matter a bit!"

Bella frowned. She didn't know much about overalls with special logos, but she guessed they took a long time to make.

"Shouldn't you have ordered them already, Mum?" she asked. "If we're opening next week, I mean?"

Suzi pulled a face. "I suppose you're right," she said. "Never mind. I'll order them now and they'll just be a few weeks late."

Bella felt all her worries coming back. Her mum was so *disorganised*. She could never do anything on time. The ironing. The phone bill. Nan's birthday present last year. It was impossible to believe that Dream Dogs would be ready. The opening party would be terrible. No customers would come.

The Dream Dogs dream was turning into a nightmare!

Fifteen minutes later, Bella, Louie and their mum were walking along the beach to school. Pepper sniffed under a row of beach huts and charged at the waves. His tail was wagging hard.

"Come on, boy!" Bella called.

Pepper backed away from one last wave and trotted over to Bella.

"Nice dog," said a voice just behind her.

Bella turned round. A tall girl with long blonde hair had appeared beside her. Bella recognised her. They were in the same class at school.

"Thanks," Bella said shyly. "His name's Pepper."

"I've got a black dog," the girl said. "He's called Snowy."

Bella giggled. "Seriously?" she said.

"Yes," the girl grinned. She had smiley blue eyes. "I guess I have a weird sense of humour.

I'm Amber. You're Bella, aren't you?"

Bella nodded.

"Have you just moved here?" Amber asked.

Bella nodded again. Then the words just came out.

"My mum's got a dog-grooming parlour called Dream Dogs," she said.

As soon as she'd said it, Bella wished she'd kept quiet about Dream Dogs.

"Wow!" Amber said. "You lucky thing. It must be brilliant. Do you get loads of dogs in all the time?"

"It hasn't opened yet," Bella admitted.

Amber's face fell. "Oh!" she said.

Bella really didn't want Amber to be

disappointed. She had high hopes that Amber could be her new best friend. "It's opening on Saturday," she said quickly. "We've got a bath for the dogs and special hairdryers and potted plants and music. Everything's pink, and our sign lights up. It's like a hairdresser's, but better."

What was she doing? Bella knew she was telling lies, but she couldn't stop.

"Fantastic," Amber gasped. "Have you given Pepper a makeover yet?"

"Not yet," Bella tumbled on. "But we'll give him one soon. Mum's ordered this special lavender dog shampoo."

"Can I bring Snowy one day?" Amber said eagerly.

Bella felt sick. "Come to the opening party on Saturday," she said. Why couldn't she *stop*? "It'll be fantastic. There'll be loads of people there. And snacks for dogs too, of course."

"Brilliant!" said Amber, her eyes sparkling.

"*Amber!*"

A woman with blonde short, spiky hair and a large black spaniel was waving at Amber.

"*Hurry up!*" the woman called. Her voice got a bit lost in the wind. "*We'll be late!*"

"Gotta go," said Amber, starting to trot away. "Mum needs to get to the shops before school. Dream Dogs sounds *really* cool! I hope we can come on Saturday! See you in class. I'll save you a seat!"

Bella watched Amber run off down the beach. She had a funny mixture of feelings in her tummy. She was pleased that Amber liked her. But at the same time, she'd never felt so worried in all her life. She'd made Dream Dogs sound amazing, but Amber was going to be

really disappointed when she found out the

truth...

Three

The Trouble with Lies...

The doorbell rang on Tuesday morning, just as Bella was finishing her breakfast. Suzi clapped her hands with excitement.

"That must be the plumber!" she said. She ran out of the kitchen towards the stairs. "Our dog bath is here!"

Bella ate her last piece of toast really quickly. "Are you coming, Louie?" she said, feeling excited as she jumped down from the table. Pepper leaped out of his basket and followed her down the stairs. What would a dog bath look like?

"Morning!" said the plumber cheerfully as Suzi, Bella, Louie and Pepper came out on to the pavement. He and his mate were lifting a long, rectangle shape out of their white van. Pepper barked furiously.

He *hated* white vans. He'd even chased one of Louie's toy vans around the carpet

once, biting it and throwing it into the air.

Bella stared at the tub.

"It's just a normal bath!" said Louie. He sounded as disappointed as Bella felt.

"Of course it is," said Suzi. She opened the front door of the salon to let the plumbers in. "We don't need anything else."

Bella followed the bath in through Dream Dogs' front door. "But I thought it would be different," she said.

"Dog-shaped or something," Louie added.

"I wanted a special bath to bathe little dogs in too," Suzi sighed. "But it was very expensive. Three thousand pounds!"

Bella tried to think of spending that kind of

money on a bath. It sounded crazy.

"That's a *lot* of footballs," said Louie.

"It certainly is," Suzi agreed.

Bella looked around Dream Dogs. She hadn't been inside the salon since Sunday. The rubbish bags were still there, and so were the paint pots. But there was something new. A high wooden platform had been built in one corner with steps leading up to it. Louie ran up the steps and jumped off the top with a shout.

"What's that, Mum?" Bella asked curiously.

"It's where we're putting our bath," Suzi explained. "It has to be high up so I won't hurt my back, washing all the dogs. Yes," she said to the plumbers, who were looking surprised. "That's right. On the top of that platform there."

Pepper sniffed at the steps. He backed away as the plumbers put the bath down on the platform. It fitted perfectly.

"Let's leave them to it," Suzi told Bella and Louie as the plumbers settled down with their tools. "Go and brush your teeth and fetch your school bags, or we'll be late!"

Bella's classroom overlooked the sea. It was strange hearing the waves crashing outside as she did her sums. The sun was shining today, and she wanted to be outside chasing the waves like Pepper.

She also wanted to be able to start her friendship with Amber all over again.

"I've told my mum about Dream Dogs," Amber told Bella at dinner time. "And she's told all her dog-walking friends. Can anyone come to the party on Saturday?"

Bella gulped. "Of course," she said. "Anyone."

"Mum's best friend Julie's got this huge Newfoundland," Amber went on. "He's

massive, like the biggest teddy bear you've ever seen. Do you think she can bring him too?"

"There's a yard out at the back," said Bella, feeling more and more miserable. "He'll be fine there."

Amber sighed. "You're so lucky," she said. "My mum and dad have got really boring jobs."

"My dad died," said Bella. At least that was true. "I don't remember him. I was only two, and my brother was a baby."

"Did he like dogs?" Amber asked.

"Yes," Bella said, remembering some of the stories her mum had told her. "Mum never had dogs until she met Dad. Now she's mad about them."

"I bet your dad would be really proud of your mum's parlour, then," said Amber.

Bella nodded. *But he wouldn't be proud of you for telling all these lies, would he?* she thought unhappily.

"Hey," said Amber, "do you think I could maybe come round later?"

Bella thought quickly. "Not today," she said. "Sorry. Um – Mum's got too much to do for the party on Saturday. Louie and I have to help her."

Amber looked disappointed. "What about Thursday?" she said.

"Don't think so," Bella whispered. Why oh *why* had she told Amber all those lies about Dream Dogs?

Amber looked a bit huffy. "Don't invite me,

then," she said. "I don't care."

Bella put her fork down. Suddenly she wasn't very hungry. Telling lies to her new friend was spoiling her appetite.

"Please don't be cross, Amber," she said. "Why don't we just play with Pepper and Snowy on the beach after school?"

Amber frowned. "I thought you had to help your mum?"

"We can do it for a bit," said Bella quickly. "And Pepper needs a walk."

Amber chewed her food for a bit. "OK," she said at last. "That sounds nice."

Bella felt relieved. Making friends was *seriously* hard work.

Suzi and Louie were waiting for Bella by the school gates at three-fifteen.

"This is my friend Amber," said Bella shyly.

Amber beamed at Suzi. "Hi!" she said. "I've heard about Dream Dogs. It sounds wicked!"

Bella gulped. She really hoped her mum wouldn't say anything about the mess that Dream Dogs was really in.

"It's going to be great," Suzi said with a smile. "Are you coming to our opening on Saturday?"

"I'll bring my mum and my dog Snowy," Amber nodded.

Amber lived further down the beach than Bella. Amber's mum and Suzi chatted together while Louie kicked his ball along. Bella found some driftwood to throw for Pepper and Snowy. Snowy was bigger and faster, and got most of the sticks first.

"Look!" Bella pointed to where Pepper and Snowy were both splashing around in the sea. "That's the first time Pepper's been in the water!"

"Snowy's used to it," said Amber. "He drank the seawater when he was a puppy, though. He was really sick."

Bella made a face. "I hope Pepper doesn't do that," she said.

Pepper and Snowy were good friends already. Bella watched them running up and down the beach, sniffing around the old beach huts and chasing each other. She wished making friends was as easy as that for her.

When Amber and her mum came to Dream Dogs on Saturday and saw what a mess the parlour was in, Amber would know Bella had lied to her. And Amber would probably never talk to her again!

Four

Making Things Worse

On Wednesday after school, Bella and Louie were helping Suzi in the parlour. The dog bath was working now, and most of the rubbish bags had gone to the dump. But nothing else had changed. The old carpet was tatty and horrible, and the walls were still green.

Louie was telling Bella and Suzi about his new friend, Jamie.

"He's into football too," he said enthusiastically. "And his dad goes to matches all the time. And he's asked if I want to go to a game with them. Can I, Mum? Please can I?"

"That sounds lovely," Suzi said. "You point Jamie out to me in the playground tomorrow. Then I'll arrange it with his mum."

Louie pulled his jumper over his head and started running around the dog parlour like he'd just scored a goal. Bella watched enviously. She really wanted to invite Amber over to play. But she couldn't.

Suzi fetched the vacuum cleaner from the

cupboard. "Amber is a nice girl, Bella," she said as she went to the plug. "Would she like to come over for tea tomorrow?"

"She's busy," Bella lied, feeling terrible. "Maybe next week."

Suzi switched on the vacuum cleaner. Pepper leaped out of his basket and ran up the stairs to the safety of the flat. Bella watched him go. Poor Pepper really hated the noise that the vacuum cleaner made.

"I'm so pleased that you're both making friends," Suzi said, raising her voice over the noise. "I know it's hard, moving to a new town. You're both doing so well. Everything's going to be great. I know it."

Bella stared at Dream Dogs' awful carpet and green walls. She swallowed. "I'll just go and check that Pepper's OK," she said. And she hurried out of the parlour and up the stairs.

She found Pepper with his nose under his paws on her bed.

"Oh, Pepper," Bella sighed. She put her cheek on Pepper's warm brown side. "I've really messed up with Amber, haven't I?"

Pepper licked her comfortingly. It made

Bella feel better. Downstairs, the vacuum cleaner had stopped.

"Come on, you scaredy cat," Bella said. "Mum wants us to help down there, not hide up here."

Bella and Pepper went back downstairs again. Bella was determined to stop worrying about Dream Dogs and start being more helpful.

She passed her mum on the stairs.

"I've just got to fetch some milk and teabags," Suzi explained. "The floor is being done tomorrow, and I need supplies in the salon's fridge for the workmen. Ooh, and I need to hang the washing on the airer as well,

or there won't be any school shirts tomorrow.
Can you keep an eye on Louie for me? I won't
be long."

In the salon, Bella tucked Pepper's favourite
blanket back into his basket. Half of it had
fallen out when Pepper had rushed upstairs. It
was old and smelly, but Pepper loved it. He
sniffed it happily and settled down again. A
white van drove past, and he shot over to the
window and barked.

"OK, Louie," said Bella, putting her hands
on her hips and staring around Dream Dogs.
"It's just you and me. What can we do to help
Mum?"

Louie wasn't listening. He'd set up a goal

between two paint pots and was firing his ball at the wall.

"Look out!" Bella shouted as his football hit one of the paint pots. The pot spun across the floor and stopped at Bella's feet. To Bella's relief, the lid stayed on the tin. But it gave her an idea.

She picked up the paint pot. The label said "Bubblegum Pink". It was a gorgeous colour, just as she had described it to 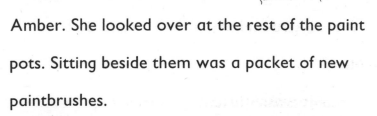 Amber. She looked over at the rest of the paint pots. Sitting beside them was a packet of new paintbrushes.

Bella eyed the big green wall at the back of the parlour. She made a decision.

"Unless we start doing something round here, Dream Dogs won't be finished by Saturday," she said, and rolled up her sleeves. "Come on, Louie. Let's start painting."

"Cool!" Louie gasped.

Bella felt excited. Maybe they *could* finish Dream Dogs by Saturday after all. The floor was being sorted out tomorrow and the dog bath was already in. How hard could painting the walls be?

"You start in that corner," she said. She opened the paint very carefully and gave Louie one of the big brushes. "I'll start over here.

We'll probably have joined it all up by the time Mum comes back down."

The first stroke of paint made Bella gasp with delight. It was delicious. The colour reminded her of her favourite pink jumper. She painted very carefully, up and down and side to side. A bit dribbled on the floor. It didn't matter, Bella decided. The old carpet was being ripped up tomorrow.

On the other side of the room, Louie had dripped paint across his shoes and across the white painted skirting board. And he wasn't painting up and down. Instead he was doing big swirls.

Bella started to feel uneasy.

51

"Don't dip the brush in so far," she said. She winced as Louie splashed bright pink paint right across his school sweatshirt. She should have gone upstairs to find some old clothes for them to wear.

"Don't boss me around, Bella," said Louie.
He loaded his brush with a big gob of pink
paint. "This is fun."

"That's way too much," Bella warned.

Louie's brush was slippery. Bella watched
with horror as it slid out of his hands. It
bounced on the ground,
sending a spray of
pink paint all over
Pepper in the window.
Pepper yelped.

"Careful!" Bella shouted.

"Sorry, Pepper!" Louie giggled.

He stepped towards Pepper. His foot caught
in the old carpet. And with a flump, Louie

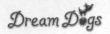

landed on his bottom, bumping into the open

paint pot.

"Oh no," Bella moaned as the paint pot

wobbled and tipped itself over.

There was pink paint *everywhere*!

Five

Trouble Bubble

Bella could hardly look at her mum as Suzi
bundled their clothes into the washing machine.

"I'm really sorry, Mum," she whispered. "I
only wanted to help."

"I know you did, Bella," Suzi said with a sigh.
She measured out the washing powder and

turned the machine on.

"Is Louie's uniform ruined?" Bella asked miserably.

"No," Suzi said. "We rinsed most of it out in the sink. I'm sure it'll come out just fine."

Louie looked disappointed. He still hated his uniform.

"It was only one pot of paint," Suzi went on. "And don't worry about the carpet. It's being ripped out tomorrow. It's Pepper we should be worrying about."

Bella looked at Pepper. The paint had dried on his back already. He looked like a stripy pink badger.

"Time for a bath, Pepper," said Suzi.

Pepper woofed as Suzi fetched a towel. Suzi went through the kitchen door to the top of the stairs. Then she stopped and looked over her shoulder.

"Well?" she said, raising her eyebrows at Bella and Louie. "Is anyone coming?"

"Is Pepper going in the new dog bath?" Bella gasped, realising where her mum was heading.

"Of course he is," said Suzi. "We need to try it out, don't we?"

Suddenly the painting disaster didn't look like such a disaster. They were going to see the new bath in action!

Bella and Louie hurried down the stairs

after their mum. Pepper woofed happily, thinking they were all going out for a walk.

"We'll shower him," Suzi said, fiddling with the taps that had been set into the wall by the bath. "And we can try some of our new lavender dog shampoo."

Bella remembered how she'd told Amber about the lavender shampoo. At least *that* hadn't been a lie. She hunted through the boxes to find the bottle that her mum wanted. Its label showed a cute photo of a dog that looked just like Pepper.

"It's a special shampoo for rough-coated dogs," Suzi explained. "It'll make Pepper's fur smoother than it's ever been!"

"Come on, boy," Bella said. She scooped Pepper up. "It'll be over really quickly, and you'll smell lovely."

She carried Pepper over to where her mum was waiting by the bath. Then she stood on tiptoe and lifted Pepper inside. Pepper sniffed the bath, but he didn't try to jump out.

"I think he likes it," said Louie.

Suzi turned on the shower attachment. Pepper stood very still as Suzi soaked him from head to foot. She put some shampoo on her hands and started working it into Pepper's back.

"You can do his legs if you want," Suzi said, offering the bottle of shampoo to Bella. "You'll have to use the steps to reach him, though."

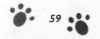

Bella could see what a good idea it had been, putting the bath up so high. Her mum was hardly bending over at all as she washed Pepper. Bella settled down on the top step and reached in to soap Pepper's paws. Louie shampooed his tail. And then Suzi turned on the shower head again and washed all the soapy suds away.

"All done," Suzi said at last, giving Pepper a pat. She stood back. "Out you get, boy."

Pepper jumped out of the tub on to the top step.

"Ugh!" Louie yelled as Pepper shook himself, covering Louie with water. Bella giggled at the cross look on her brother's face.

"I'll dry him!" Bella said.

She grabbed the towel and dried Pepper all over, rubbing his face gently and his tummy a little harder. Louie opened the front door to let out some of the steam that had filled the parlour.

"Now for the fun part," said Suzi, looking excited. Opening the cupboard, she pulled out a

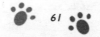

big hairdryer. It was the same shape as a
normal one, but it was on a stand and was
about three times bigger. "This arrived this
morning," she said proudly. "It's specially made
for dogs. It'll dry Pepper in no time."

She went to plug the hairdryer in. Bella
frowned.

"Mum," she began. "Pepper hates..."

It was too late. The hairdryer roared into
life. It sounded just like the vacuum cleaner.

Pepper leaped up. The door to the flat was closed. But the front door to the salon was open. Before Bella could stop him, Pepper had wriggled away from her and shot outside. Suzi gasped.

"Pepper!" Bella cried in dismay. She jumped up and ran to the door. Louie followed. "Pepper, come back!" she called. Then she ran outside, the towel still in her hand. "Pepper!" she shouted helplessly.

"Where's he gone?" Louie asked, coming out with Bella.

Suzi rushed past them both. "Excuse me?" Bella heard her asking some of the late-afternoon shoppers. "Did you see a little brown

dog just now? About as high as my knee?"

Bella watched as people shook their heads and continued on their way. She ran up and grabbed her mum's arm. "It's really dark," she said anxiously. "Pepper doesn't know Sandmouth very well, and he'll be cold because he's wet."

"Oh dear," said Suzi. Her eyes filled with tears. "This is all my fault. I was so keen to try out my new dryer that I forgot how much Pepper would hate the noise."

"He can't be far away," Bella said, trying to sound positive. "Come on! Let's look for him!"

Suzi hesitated. "You'll need your coats," she said at last. "Hats too. I'll fetch them. And a torch. Oh, poor Pepper! I hope he's all right!"

Six

Where's Pepper?

Bella could feel her eyes closing. She had hardly slept last night but she couldn't go to sleep in her classroom. She'd get into trouble.

Mr Evans the teacher was showing them something on the whiteboard. Bella hoped he wasn't going to ask her any questions. She hadn't been listening at all.

"Hey, Bella!" Amber whispered at her. "Are you OK?"

Bella shook her head. She could feel the tears coming to her eyes. She swallowed and pushed them back as hard as she could.

"Pepper's run away," she told Amber.

Amber looked shocked. "What? When?" she gasped.

"Last night," Bella said.

"Bella?" said Mr Evans sharply. "Amber? Stop talking, please."

A tear escaped and ran down Bella's cheek. Mr Evans looked worried. He was a nice teacher. Everyone in the school liked him.

"Is everything all right, Bella?" he asked in his soft Welsh accent.

"She's lost her dog, sir," said Amber, putting her arm round Bella.

The rest of Class Three looked round. Everyone looked really sorry to hear Bella's news.

"Oh!" said Mr Evans, frowning even more. "I'm so sorry. What happened?"

"We washed him but Pepper didn't like the noise of Mum's new dryer," Bella gulped. "He ran outside. We looked *everywhere*. We didn't go to bed till ten o'clock. And I didn't sleep at all because I was really worried about him."

The class murmured. Mr Evans found Bella

some tissues so she could blow her nose. "I'm sure your mum will find him," he reassured Bella. "I expect Pepper will be at the gates, waiting for you at the end of the day. How about that?"

The thought of Pepper waiting at the end of school comforted Bella. She stopped crying.

"Bella's mum has a new dog parlour called Dream Dogs, Mr Evans," said Amber.

Bella shrank down in her chair. She knew Amber was trying to help. The trouble was, she was doing completely the opposite.

"It's opening on Saturday," Amber continued. "You could bring your dog."

Mr Evans looked surprised. "How do you

know I've got a dog, Amber?" he asked.

Amber flicked her plaits back over her shoulders. "There's dog hair on your trousers," she said.

Mr Evans looked down. Sure enough, there were pale dog hairs on his black trousers. The class giggled. Even Bella smiled a little. It was funny, seeing Mr Evans's face.

"You're right," Mr Evans said. "I've got a big golden retriever called Barney. Perhaps you should be a detective when you're older, Amber!"

"You should bring Barney to Dream Dogs on Saturday, sir," said Amber. She looked at the rest of the class. "Everyone who's got a dog is welcome. That's right, isn't it, Bella?"

Bella nodded helplessly. Everyone in the class was looking at her with new interest.

"We've got a Staffy called Tubs," said Ryan, a boy near the front of the room.

"We've got two dachshunds!"

"My nan's got a collie..."

Suddenly everyone was talking about their

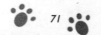

dogs. Mr Evans clapped his hands for silence. Slowly, the class stopped chattering and started concentrating on the lesson again.

"I'm sure Mr Evans is right about Pepper," Amber whispered, nudging Bella. "He'll be with your mum at the end of school. I know it!"

When the bell rang for the end of school, Bella ran out of her classroom with her heart thumping.

"Walk, please, Bella!" Mr Evans called. "Hope everything's OK with Pepper!"

Bella forced herself to walk. Amber walked beside her, chattering confidently about Pepper.

"He'll be there, I know it, Bella! It'll be great! He'll jump up and lick you..."

Bella strained her eyes to see if her mum and Pepper were at the gate. She could see her mum's brown hair. But the crowd was too thick to spot Pepper.

"You'll have to wash him again," Amber continued. "Dogs like rolling in smelly things when they run away." She looked hopefully at Bella. "Can I come and help wash him?"

"Course you can," said Bella, without thinking.

Amber looked thrilled. "Excellent!" she said happily.

Before Bella had time to regret inviting

Amber back, her mum stepped out of the crowd.

"Hi, love," she said.

Suzi's eyes were red. Louie was scuffing the ground with his toes and wouldn't look at Bella. Pepper wasn't with them.

"I'm sorry," Suzi gulped, stroking Louie's head. "We haven't found Pepper. I looked as long as I could. I even went round asking white-van drivers if a little brown dog had barked at them or chased them. But there's been so much going on at Dream Dogs I kept having to go back to let people in and out. I looked, really I did."

For once, Amber was silent. Bella felt numb.

Pepper had truly disappeared.

"I'll come back with you, shall I?" Amber said at last. "I'm sure Mum would—"

All the worry about Pepper and Dream Dogs and all the lies she'd told suddenly got too much for Bella.

"No!" she shouted. "You can't come back! Not ever!"

Amber's mouth fell open. Louie and Suzi both looked shocked.

"Bella, that's not very nice—" Suzi began.

"I wish everyone would leave me alone!" Bella yelled.

Amber had gone red. "You're the most horrible person I've ever met, Bella," she shouted back. "I'm not surprised your dog ran away!"

Amber stormed off. Feeling terrible, Bella watched her go.

"If Jamie talked to me like that," said Louie after a minute, "I wouldn't want to be friends with him either."

"Louie's got a point," Suzi said. "What was that about, Bella?"

"Oh, Mum," Bella whispered. "I've made such a mess of everything." And she burst into tears.

Seven

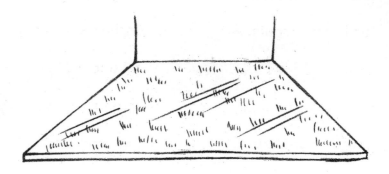

Friends Again?

By Friday the Dream Dogs parlour had a
brilliant new floor. It looked like a huge
photograph of a garden lawn had been stuck
down on the floor.

"It's just like grass!" said Louie, jumping up
and down.

"I want the dogs to feel at home," said Suzi.

Bella thought her mum looked tired. She knew Suzi had been out half the night looking for Pepper again. But Pepper's basket was still empty, and his food bowl was still untouched.

"Hope the dogs don't do poos on it, Mum," Louie sniggered, still staring at the grass-style floor. He held his nose and danced around.

"Shut up, Louie," Bella snapped. "Don't you even *care* about Pepper?"

Suzi rubbed her eyes. "Don't fight, kids," she said wearily. "And don't say 'shut up', Bella. It's not nice. I don't understand what's the matter with you at the moment."

Bella hadn't explained her argument with

Amber. When her mum had asked her about it, she'd just clamped her mouth shut. Suzi had given up after a bit. But she kept looking at Bella in this worried way. Bella wished she could explain everything. But somehow, she couldn't.

"Bella's horrible," Louie chanted, and stuck his tongue out at Bella. "Bella's horrible!"

I won't cry, Bella thought fiercely to herself. She was tired of feeling miserable all the time. Feeling bad wasn't going to help her find Pepper, or make it up with Amber, or get Dream Dogs ready on time. Bella tried not to think about the parlour's tatty walls, which looked worse than ever thanks to her and Louie and the pink paint. Instead, she thought of all the good things about Dream Dogs. The floor looked fantastic, and all the rubbish bags had disappeared. And the wall beside the bath had been covered in smart white tiles.

Thinking about the good things stopped the tears from coming. But Bella still felt bad.

"Apologise to Louie, Bella," Suzi ordered.

"I'm sorry, Louie," Bella said.

Louie shrugged. "I'm sorry too," he said. "I do care about Pepper. I'm just making jokes so I feel better."

Suzi locked the door and they all set off

towards the beach. Louie met his friend Jamie almost at once, and the boys ran down the beach with Louie's football. Bella wasn't sure if she wanted to meet Amber or not. She had to tell Amber the truth about Dream Dogs if she wanted to be friends with her again. And that was going to be really hard.

"We've got lots of shopping to do for the party tomorrow afternoon," said Suzi, slipping her arm through Bella's. "We need to get in some wine and other drinks for the guests. And crisps and things like that."

"Don't forget the snacks for the dogs," Bella said, remembering what she'd told Amber.

Suzi gasped. "Of course!" she said. "We'll

get some nice doggie treats, and make the yard all safe and nice with toys and bowls of water."

"Pepper would love it," Bella said sadly.

Suzi squeezed Bella's arm. "That's the problem, isn't it, love?" she said. "You're missing Pepper. I'm sure Amber would understand."

Bella just nodded.

"We'll find Pepper," Suzi promised. "I've

done flyers and I'm going to put them up all over Sandmouth while you're at school. There're only a couple of deliveries for Dream Dogs today, so I'll have more time."

Up ahead, Bella saw Amber's red-gold plaits. She took a deep breath.

"Sorry, Mum," she said. "I have to talk to Amber."

Suzi nodded. "Good girl," she said. "You have to face up to things to make them better, don't you?"

Bella jogged down the beach, thinking about what her mum had said. Problems always got worse, the longer you left them. She understood that now.

"Amber!" she called. "Amber, wait!"

Amber stopped and turned round. Her arms were folded tightly across her tummy.

"What do you want?" Amber said.

"I want to say sorry," Bella said bravely. "I was really upset about Pepper."

Amber dropped her arms. "Have you found him?" she asked.

Bella shook her head. "Mum's going to look again today," she said. "And Louie and I will help her look after school again too, if she hasn't found him by home time. But Amber? That's not all."

Amber frowned.

"I've been very stupid," Bella said. She

swallowed. "You see, it's not just about Pepper.
I lied about Dream Dogs."

Amber looked surprised. "What do you
mean?" she said. "Your mum *doesn't* have a dog
parlour?"

"She does," Bella said, "but it's not finished.
It isn't pink, and it doesn't have lovely plants
everywhere, and it doesn't have music. It's a bit
of a mess, actually."

"I don't understand," Amber said.

Bella stared at the sand under her feet. "I lied about it so you'd like me," she said. "You were so interested when we talked about it. I thought maybe you wouldn't like me if I told you the truth. And I didn't want to invite you back because you'd see that I'd been lying all along. And I got in a total mess about everything because I want to be friends with you."

Amber was quiet. Bella walked beside her, wondering what Amber would say.

"Is the party tomorrow real?" Amber asked at last.

Bella nodded. "We're shopping for food and

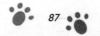

drinks tomorrow morning," she said. "And there is a yard out the back for the dogs. It'll probably be good fun if lots of people come and don't mind too much about the mess. Just — don't expect it to look like I said."

She looked hopefully at Amber. Was she going to forgive her?

"What about the sign?" said Amber.

"Oh, the sign's real," said Bella. "It's really bright and really pink. You turn it on with this switch inside."

"Can I turn it on sometime?" Amber asked.

Bella stared down at where Amber had linked arms with her. She knew right then that everything was going to be fine.

"Course you can," she said gratefully.
"Come over later, if you like. You can turn it
on after school."

Amber shook her head.

Bella felt worried. "Why not?" she asked.

"Because we're going to look for Pepper
after school," said Amber. "Aren't we?"

Eight

Detective Work

By home time on Friday, Pepper still hadn't been found.

"So you really looked *everywhere?*" Bella asked her mum desperately.

"Everywhere I could think of," Suzi said, shaking her head. "Do you think we should cancel the Dream Dogs party tomorrow? It won't feel right without Pepper."

"Don't cancel it, Mum," Bella said. "Pepper wouldn't want us to."

Suzi looked uncertain. "I suppose you're right," she said. "It's just — I bought Pepper a new collar specially for the party..."

"Don't cry," said Bella quickly as her mum started sniffing. "Amber's going to help us look for Pepper. Aren't you, Amber?"

Amber nodded. "I'm a bit of a detective," she said. "I might think of something you haven't thought of yet."

"Yes!" Bella said, remembering how Amber had guessed about Mr Evans's dog. "Amber's

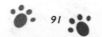

brilliant at detective work!"

"So, Detective Amber," Suzi said with a watery smile as they all walked away from the school gates towards the beach. "What should we do?"

"Look for clues," Amber said. "And also it's important to get as much information as possible. What does Pepper like?"

"Bones," said Suzi. "Cuddles. Oh, and walks, of course."

"He likes walking on the beach," Bella said.

"Whereabouts?" Amber asked.

The tide was going out. Louie went down to the water's edge to look for pawprints. Bella gazed around.

"He's still a bit scared of the sea," she said

at last, thinking hard. She looked up to where the beach met the seafront and the main road in and out of Sandmouth. "But he liked sniffing around the beach huts further along."

Amber's eyes gleamed. Then she raced off.

Bella suddenly felt excited. Amber was going to find Pepper for them! She ran after Amber as her friend ran towards the beach huts.

Most of the huts were closed up for the winter. Amber tried the door of the first one. As Bella hunted underneath where the hut stood up on its stilts, Amber ran to the second hut. Bella raced past her, heading for a blue hut that she remembered Pepper sniffing at a few days earlier.

She stopped at the sight of a clump of rough brown fur caught on the edge of one of the blue hut's stilts.

"Over here!" Bella shouted.

Suzi, Louie and Amber rushed towards Bella as she rattled the door of the beach hut. It was locked.

"Pepper!" she called, trying to peer under the door.

There was a weak bark. Bella felt the thump on the wood as something hurled itself at the door. She burst into tears.

Pepper was locked inside!

"Pepper!" she called as Pepper barked and jumped against the door. "It's OK, boy. We'll get you out!"

"Down here!" Suzi shouted from beneath the hut. "There're some loose boards. Looks like they push inwards. Pepper must have pushed inside, but couldn't push his way out again!"

Bella crawled underneath the hut. Amber and Louie were already there with Suzi. They all pushed and heaved at the broken boards.

Bella could see Pepper's brown nose. Then she

felt his solid body. And then his pink tongue

was everywhere, licking them all from head to

foot. Bella felt his paws round her neck as he

cuddled her as hard as he could.

"We've got you, Pepper," Bella laughed into

his brown fur. "You're safe!"

Louie threw his arms round Pepper. "And you *stink*!" he added, pulling a face.

"Bath time," Bella grinned as Pepper licked her ears. "And no hairdryers this time. We promise!"

Nine

Party Time!

It was Saturday at last! Bella opened the door

and grinned out at Amber. Amber stopped trying

to look through the cracks on the big blinds that

were drawn down over the Dream Dogs' window.

"Why are the blinds down?" Amber asked.

"We don't want to spoil the surprise," said

Bella, moving across the doorway to block Amber's view inside. "Not till the guests arrive."

"I *am* a guest," Amber said indignantly. "So why won't you let me see?"

Bella wrinkled her nose. "Well," she said. "You are a bit early. The party doesn't start for another twenty minutes."

"Stop teasing Amber, Bella!" Suzi called from inside. "Tell her she can come in. Is your mum there, Amber?"

"She's just coming with Snowy and Joe, my brother," Amber called back. "Come on, Bella," she said, trying to wriggle past. "Let me in!"

Bella giggled. "Well," she said, opening the

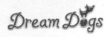
Dream Dogs' parlour door very slowly. "Like I said, don't expect miracles, OK?"

Amber rolled her eyes. "I know what to expect," she said. "I was over here washing Pepper with you last night, wasn't I?"

Amber stepped through the door. Her eyes widened.

"But it's finished!" she gasped. "It's just the way you first described it!"

The walls of Dream Dogs were bright pink. The shelves groaned with neatly folded towels and rows of dog products. Spider plants and peace lilies hung in baskets from the ceiling. Soft music played from a speaker in one high corner of the room. A row of dog-lead hooks were neatly screwed to the wall beside the

door. There were four small dog cages under

the plush window bench, and a fence with a

dog-gate stood between the front door and the

rest of the parlour.

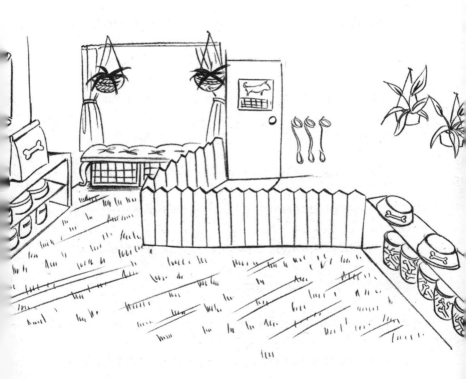

"Just in case any of our customers try to run away like Pepper did," said Suzi, smiling as she dried her hands on one of the towels.

Bella burst out laughing at the look on Amber's face. "Mum was up all night painting the walls," she said. "We put the shelves up at nine o'clock this morning, and then we did the dog fence. And the plants arrived half an hour ago. Look – they're still dripping from where Mum watered them!"

Amber's mum and brother arrived at the door. They were a bit breathless. It looked like Snowy had pulled them the whole way.

"You can take Snowy out to the yard," Suzi said to Amber's mum and brother. "There're toys and goodies for the dogs. I'll sort out some drinks for you."

Pepper jumped up from his basket and frisked around Snowy's black legs. The two dogs woofed at each other and charged out of the back door.

"Can I open the crisps yet, Mum?" Louie shouted from the top of the stairs.

"Yes!" Suzi called back. "Put them in the bowls I've laid out. But don't eat them!

"This place is awesome," Amber said, turning round to look at everything. "It really is, Bella. I thought it was pretty cool last night, but now..."

"You haven't seen the best bit yet," said Bella. She grabbed her friend's hand. "Let's lift the blinds first. Then we'll do the sign."

Together, the girls went to the window and pulled up the blinds. The parlour flooded with light, making the pink walls look even pinker.

Outside, Amber and Bella saw Mr Evans heading towards the parlour with his big golden retriever on a lead. Not far behind him was

Ryan from Class Three with Tubs, his
Staffordshire terrier. Soon the whole parlour
would be full, the party would begin – and
Dream Dogs would be well and truly open.

"Quick," Bella gasped. "The sign!"

She showed Amber where the switch was.
Then Bella went outside, just like her mum had
done the week before.

"OK!" she called to Amber through her
cupped hands. "Turn it on!"

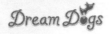

The pink curly sign shimmered to life above the gleaming window. Dream Dogs was open for business.

Top tips from vets!

If you are worried about your dog running away, like Pepper, there are some simple things you can do to keep your dog safe.

- **Make sure your dog wears a collar and tag when outside – this is the law.**
- **Keep your dog on a lead when out for a walk if there is any chance they could get lost or hurt themselves.**
- **Train your dog to come to you when you call their name.**
- **Get your dog microchipped so they can be easily identified if they do run off.**

Did you know?

A microchip can be harmlessly injected by your vet into the scruff of their neck and it's scanned like a barcode to reveal their owner's details.

For more tips on pet care, great competitions and games visit www.pdsa.org.uk/petprotectors

for pets in need of vets

Dream Dogs

SASHA

Bella is in big trouble. Two identical white pooches came to the Dream Dogs parlour before an important dog show. But the dogs have got mixed up and Bella can't tell which is Sasha and which is Silky!

Will Bella get the right dogs back to their owners before the show starts?

Read on for a sneak preview of the next Dream Dogs adventure...

Bella picked up Silky. The dog was as light as a feather. Then she opened the door that led to the flat's staircase. Amber was hiding in the hallway with Sasha. Bella felt Silky stiffen.

"Wrow!" barked Silky in a little high voice.

"Wrow! Wrow!"

"Wrow!" Sasha barked back.

"Shh!" Bella hissed helplessly. Mrs Lockett would hear!

Sasha was now growling too. The two dogs obviously hated each other.

"Oh!" Amber squealed as Sasha wriggled out of her grasp and jumped to the floor.

The sight of her enemy gave Silky extra strength. She pushed herself out of Bella's arms and jumped down as well. Sasha and Silky started running round each other, nipping at each other's legs and growling squeakily.

"Um, Bella?" said Amber in a strange voice. "Which dog is which?"

Bella stared at the two bichon frises. Neither of them had their collars on. Both of them were girls. Both of them were white and fluffy... and completely identical.

"I don't know," said Bella in dismay.

She looked from Silky one dog to the other, and back again. The more she looked, the more confused she felt.

"Oh no!" Amber squealed. "What are we going to do?"

Take home all of the
Dream Dogs

If you have it, tick it!

Available now:

Out in May:

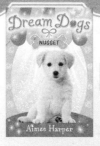

Out in July: